Beauty
AND THE
BEAST

and other stories

Beauty
AND THE
BEAST

and other stories

Retold by Adèle Geras

Illustrated by Louise Brierley

VIKING

Published by the Penguin Group
27 Wrights Lane, London W8 5TZ, England
Penguin Books USA Inc, 375 Hudson Street, New York, New York 10014, USA
Penguin Books Australia Ltd, Ringwood, Victoria, Australia
Penguin Books Canada Ltd, 10 Alcorn Avenue, Toronto, Ontario, Canada, M4V 3B2
Penguin Books (NZ) Ltd, 182-190 Wairau Road, Auckland 10, New Zealand

Penguin Books Ltd, Registered Offices: Harmondsworth, Middlesex, England

First published 1996

Text copyright ©1996 by Adèle Geras
Illustrations copyright ©1996 by Louise Brierley

1 3 5 7 9 10 8 6 4 2

British Library Cataloguing in Publication Data
CIP data for this book is available from the British Library

ISBN 0-670-86652-0

Printed by Imago

CONTENTS

∾

BEAUTY AND THE BEAST

A very long time ago, in a distant land, there lived a merchant. His wife had been dead for many years, but he had three daughters and the youngest was so lovely that everyone who saw her wondered at her beauty. Her name was Belle, and she was as good and kind a child as any man could wish for. When a storm at sea sank all but one of the merchant's ships, the family was left with very little money, and Belle was the only one of the three sisters who never complained.

"We shall have to clean the house now," sighed the eldest. "And cook as well, I daresay."

"No more pretty new clothes for us," moaned the second sister. "And no maid to dress our hair each morning and prepare our baths each night."

"We are young and strong," said Belle, "and we shall manage perfectly well until Father's last ship comes to port."

"You are a silly goose" said the older girls. "Hoping when there is so very little hope. The last ship probably went down with all the rest, taking our wealth with it."

Spring turned to summer, and towards the end of summer came news that the merchant's last ship had indeed been saved and was now docked in the small harbour of a town not three days' ride from his house.

"I shall set out at once," he said, "and return within the week. Fortune has smiled on us at last, and I am in the mood to celebrate. What gifts shall I bring you, daughters, from the grand shops that I shall surely see on my journey?"

"Something that sparkles like a star," said the eldest. "A diamond, I think."

"Something that glows like a small moon," said the second daughter. "A pearl to hang around my neck."

Belle said nothing.

"And you, my little one," said the merchant. "What would delight your heart?"

"To see you safely back in this house after your travels would please me more than anything," said Belle. "But if I have to choose a gift, then what I should like is one red rose."

As soon as the merchant finished his business in the harbour, he set off for home. His saddle-bags were filled with gold coins, for he had sold everything that had been on board the last of his ships. Even after buying a diamond for one daughter and a pearl for another, there was plenty of money left.

"But," he said to himself, "there are no red roses anywhere in the town. I must look about me as I ride, and perhaps I shall see one growing wild."

The merchant made his way home, lost in daydreams of how he would spend his new-found wealth. Dusk fell and soon the poor man realized that he had strayed from the roadway and that his horse was making its way down a long avenue of black trees towards some lights that were shining in the distance.

"This must be a nobleman's country estate," said the merchant to himself. Through tall wrought-iron gates, he saw the finest mansion he had ever laid eyes on. There was a lamp burning at every window.

Having no one else to talk to, the merchant said to his horse, "The gentleman to whom all this belongs is at home, beyond a doubt, and a large party of guests with him, it would seem. Perhaps he will extend his hospitality to one who has strayed from his path. Come, my friend. I will dismount and we will walk together up this handsome drive."

The gates opened as the merchant touched them. When he reached the front door, he said to his horse, "Wait here for a moment, while I announce myself."

He stepped over the threshold, but there was no one there to greet him, and a thick white silence filled every corner of the vast hall.

"Is anyone here?" cried the merchant, and his own voice came back to him, echoing off the high walls.

He went outside again quickly and said to his horse, "Come, we will find the stable, my friend, for everyone in the house seems to have disappeared. Still, it is a beautiful place. Perhaps I shall find a maid in the kitchen who will give me a morsel of food and show me a bed where I may spend the night, for we shall never find our way back to the highway in the dark."

The stable was comfortable and clean, and the merchant fed his horse, and settled him in one of the empty stalls.

Then he returned to the house, thinking that by now someone would have appeared.

There was no one to be seen, but a delicious smell of food hung in the air. Yes, thought the merchant, that door, which was shut, is now open, and someone is serving a meal.

He walked into this new room and saw one place laid at a long table. He saw a flagon of wine and one glass, and many china plates bearing every sort of delicacy a person could desire.

"Is there anyone here to join me in this feast?" said the merchant to the embroidered creatures looking down at him from the tapestries on the walls, but there was no reply, so he sat down at the table and ate and drank his fill.

"I think," he said aloud, "that I have come to an enchanted dwelling, and I shall now take this candlestick and see what lies upstairs. Perhaps a kind fairy has made a bed ready for me, and a bath as well."

He went upstairs, and saw that there, too, the lamps had been lit, so that he had no need of his candle. He opened the first door on a long corridor and found himself in the most sumptuous of bedrooms. The sheets were made of silk, and soft towels had been laid out on the bed. He could see curls of steam drifting from an adjoining chamber, and as he pushed open the door, he discovered a bath, ready for him to step into.

"Whoever you are," said the merchant to the velvet curtains that had been drawn across the windows, "you are the most thoughtful of hosts. I can smell the lavender oil you have sprinkled in the bath . . . Maybe in the morning you will show yourself and I will be able to thank you properly."

The merchant bathed and went to bed and fell into a dreamless sleep. When he woke up, the curtains had been pulled back, the sun was shining, and a tray with his breakfast upon it had been placed on a small table near the window. A fine set of clothes had been prepared for him, and he put it on and marvelled at how well it fitted. At first he could not find his own travel-stained garments, but they had been washed and dried and pressed and lay folded beside his saddle-bags, which he had left beside the front door the previous night.

"I must go home," he thought to himself. "However pleasant this place may be, I must return to my children. I shall fetch my horse from the stable and set off at once."

The gardens of the mansion were a small paradise. Seeing them spread out before him reminded the merchant that he still had not found a red rose for Belle.

"In this garden," he thought, "there may still be red roses, even though autumn is nearly upon us. I shall pick just one, if I see some, and be gone."

Flowers still bloomed in the garden, but the merchant had to walk along many paths before he came to a bush covered with red roses, that had just blossomed. He chose the plumpest and smoothest; the most luscious and velvety of all the flowers he could see, and snapped it off the bush.

At that moment, an anguished roar filled the air and there, towering over him, was the most hideous creature the merchant had ever seen; a being from the worst of his nightmares; something that could not be human even though it stood upright and wore a man's clothes and spoke in a man's voice.

"Ungrateful wretch!" this Beast said. "All that I have done for you: fed you and clothed you and sheltered you . . . all that is not enough. No, you must steal a bud from my most precious rosebush. There is no punishment but death for

such ingratitude."

The merchant began to weep.

"I did not mean it as theft," he said. "The owner of this place – you – I knew how kind you must be. I thought a rosebud was but a trifling thing after all the wonders you had lavished on me. It is a present for my youngest daughter. I promised her a red rose before I set out on my journey, or I would never have touched anything that belonged to you. I beg you, spare my life."

"You must not judge by appearances," said the Beast. "I love my roses more than anything in the world, and a red rose is no trifling thing to me. Now you have plucked one for your child. I will spare your life, but only on this condition. One of your daughters must return with you in a month's time, and you must leave her here for ever. She must come of her own free will, and bear whatever fate awaits her in this place. If none of your children will make this sacrifice for you, then you yourself must return and be punished for your crime. Go now. I will wait for you and for whichever daughter may choose to accompany you."

When the merchant reached his home, he wept as he told the story of the enchanted mansion and of what he had promised the Beast. His two elder daughters glanced first at the jewelled necklaces he had brought them and then at one another, but not a word did they utter.

Belle smiled and said, "Dry your tears, Father. It was for the sake of my red rose that you ventured into the garden, so I shall go with you and with pleasure."

The cold came early that autumn. As Belle and her father made their way back to the Beast's mansion, snow began to fall, and by the time they reached the wrought-iron gates, it seemed as though white sheets had been spread over the whole landscape. The merchant's heart was like a stone in his breast, and Belle was trying to cheer him as they drew near the house.

"You must not worry about me, Father, for if you do, it will make me very unhappy. I know that my happiness is your dearest wish, so for my sake, let your spirits be high. I want to remember you smiling." Belle smiled at her father, as if to set him an example. She said, "This is a very handsome building, and from all that you told me about the Master of this place, he seems to be a kind and hospitable creature. I do not see anything so terrible in living here, if your life is to be spared as a consequence."

"You have not seen the Beast," said the merchant, shivering. "Oh, you will change your tune when you do, my dear."

The door opened at their touch, just as it had before.

"We have come," the merchant called out, "as I promised."

His words floated up towards the ceiling, but no one appeared.

"Come," said the merchant. "Let us go into the banqueting hall and eat, for we have had a long journey, and you must be hungry, my dear."

Two places had been set at the table. Belle and her father were eating with heavy hearts when the Beast came silently into the room. It was only when he spoke that Belle caught sight of him, hidden in the shadows by the door.

"Is this the daughter," said the Beast, "who comes here in your place?"

"Yes, I am," Belle answered for her father. "My name is Belle and I am happy to be in such a beautiful house, and happy to be of service to my father."

"You will not be so happy," said the Beast, "once you have looked upon my face. It will fill you with horror and haunt all your dreams."

For her father's sake, Belle knew she had to be brave. She said, "I have heard your voice, sir, and it is as low and sweet a voice as any man ever spoke with. Your face holds no terrors for me."

The Beast stepped out of the shadows by the door, and the light of all the lamps in the room fell on his face. Belle's hands flew to cover her eyes, to shield them from the hideous sight, and it was with great difficulty that at last she peeped between her fingers at the Beast.

"Now," he said, "are you as ready as you were a moment ago to spend your days with me?"

Belle was quiet for a full minute, then she said, "I will become used to looking at you, sir, and then I will not flinch as I did just now. You must forgive me for my cruelty. It was the unexpectedness of seeing you for the first time. I shall not hide my eyes again."

The Beast bowed. "You are as kind as you are beautiful. Everything I own, everything in this place is yours to do with as you will. I shall keep out of your sight, except for one hour in the evening, when I will come into the drawing-room for some conversation. For the present, I beg the two of you to enjoy this last night together, for tomorrow your father must leave and return home. I bid you both goodnight."

The next morning, after her father had gone, Belle wept for a long time. Then she dried her eyes and said to herself, "Crying will not help me, nor despair. I must strive to enjoy everything there is to enjoy, and find the courage to endure whatever I have to endure."

She decided to explore the mansion, and found that everything she looked at had been designed to please her. There were books in the library, a piano in the music room, paints and pencils for her amusement, a wardrobe full of the most beautiful clothes that anyone could wish for, and everywhere invisible hands that made all ready for her and smoothed her way.

Beside her bed, on a small table, there lay a looking-glass and a note which read:

"Whatever you may wish to see
will in this glass reflected be."

Belle picked up the little mirror and wished that she might see her family and know how they fared, but the images that appeared made her so homesick, that at once she put the glass away in a drawer and tried to forget all about it.

And so Belle passed her days pleasantly enough, and every evening as the clock struck nine, the Beast came and sat beside her in the drawing-room.

At first, Belle dreaded this time, and the sound of the Beast's footsteps on the marble floors made her tremble with fear. But when he sat down, his face was in shadow, and as they talked, Belle's fears melted away, and the hour passed too quickly. Soon, she began to long for the evening, and to wish that she might spend time with the Beast during the day.

One night, as the candles guttered and flickered, the Beast stood up to take his leave of her.

Belle whispered, "Stay a little longer, sir. It is very lonely and quiet without you, and this hour is so short."

The Beast sat down again, and said, "I will gladly stay for as long as you wish, but there is a question I must ask you and I shall ask this question every night and you must answer me honestly."

"I would never lie to you, sir," said Belle, "for you are the best and most generous of creatures."

"Then tell me, Belle, would you consent to marry me?"

"Oh, no, sir!" cried Belle, and her hands flew to her mouth and she

shuddered in disgust. "No, I could never marry you. I am sorry to say this after all your kindness to me, but oh, no, do not ask such a thing of me, I implore you!"

The Beast turned away from the light.

"I apologize for causing you distress," he said, "but I must ask this question every night."

Time went by. Belle and the Beast spoke of everything: of dreams and songs and poems and flowers and wars and noble deeds and merriment. They spoke of wizards and dragons and magic and marvels, of clouds and mountains and distant empires. They discussed kings and emperors, architecture and farming, families and animals. The only subject they never mentioned was love.

And still, as he left her side, the Beast asked every night, "Will you marry me, Belle?" and Belle would say that she could not.

At first she said it in words, but gradually, uttering the syllables that hurt the Beast so much began to hurt her, too, and she found herself unable to speak. After that, she simply shook her head and her heart grew heavier and heavier.

One night, after Belle had spent nearly a year and a half in the Beast's house, she took the enchanted mirror out of the drawer, and asked to be shown her family at home. What she saw was an old man lying sick and feverish in his bed. She could scarcely recognize her dear father, who had been so tall and strong and who had seemed to her so young. She wept bitterly at the sight.

"I shall ask the Master to let me visit him," she decided. "He would not refuse me such a favour."

That evening, Belle wept again as she told the Beast of her father's illness.

"If you let me go to him, I promise to come back within the week, only I cannot bear to see him suffering."

"And I cannot bear to see *you* suffering, my dear one. Take this magic ring with you, and place it on your finger when you wish to return to this place. All you have to do to be in your father's house is look into the mirror and wish yourself transported."

"Thank you, thank you, dear sir," said Belle. "I shall be back with you before you can miss me."

"And will you marry me, dearest Belle?"

"No, sir," said Belle. "You know I could never do that."

"Then goodnight," said the Beast, "and may you find whatever it is you seek."

The next morning, Belle woke up in her father's house. His happiness at her return was so great that his health immediately improved, and even Belle's sisters were glad to see her. But every night at nine o'clock, Belle found her thoughts turning to the Beast, and she missed their conversations together and their shared laughter.

When the week was over, she was quite ready to leave, but her father's piteous tears persuaded her and she agreed to stay with her family for a few more days. "The Master will not mind," she said to herself, "for he is so kind and gentle."

On the third night of the second week, Belle dreamed of the rose garden. She saw in her dream the very bush from which her father had taken the red rose she had asked for, and under the bush lay the Master. His voice came to her from far away.

"I am dying, Belle," she heard. "Dying for love of you. I cannot live even one more day if you do not come back. You have broken your promise to me, and thus broken my heart . . ."

Belle awoke from the dream at once, cold and terrified.

Quickly, she put on the magic ring and lay back against the pillows.

"Take me back to him," she told the ring, and tears poured from her eyes. "What if I am too late and my Master is dead? Oh, let me be in time. Please let me be in time!"

Belle opened her eyes and she was once more in her bedroom in the mansion. Without even pausing to put slippers on her feet, she ran through the corridors and down the stairs and out of the front door. Breathless, she came to the rose garden, and there on the ground lay the Beast, silent and unmoving. Belle flung herself upon him and took him in her arms.

"Oh, Master, please, please do not die. I cannot, I cannot be too late. How will I ever bear it if you die? Oh, can you not feel my love for you? Come back to life and I will do anything . . . I will marry you gladly, joyously – only speak to me, I beseech you."

Belle's tears fell on the Beast's hair as she kissed his eyes and clasped him to her heart. At last he stirred and Belle looked down at him for the first time. She found she was embracing a handsome young man, and recoiled at once.

"You are not my beloved Master," she cried. "Where is he? I love him. I want to marry him."

"Don't you recognize me?" asked the young man, who indeed did speak with the Beast's own voice. "Don't you know me without the mask of my ugliness? It is I, and you will never call me Master again, but Husband and Friend. I am the same as I ever was, and love you as much as I ever did. You have released me from a dreadful spell laid upon me in childhood by a wicked fairy who was envious of my wealth. She turned me into a monster until the day a woman would agree to marry me. Can you love me, Belle, as I really am?"

"I will love you," said Belle. "I *do* love you. I have loved you for a long time, though I did not realize it until last night. I love your face, whether it be beautiful or hideous, for it is your face and only an outer shell for your honourable soul."

"Then we shall be happy for ever," said the young man. "And the whole world will dance at our wedding."

Belle smiled and took his hand, and they entered their home together.

HANSEL AND GRETEL

❧

The harvest had failed and there was hunger in the land. It is hard to fall asleep when you have eaten no supper, and Hansel and Gretel lay upstairs in their small bedroom, listening to the voices floating up through cracks in the wooden floorboards.

"If there were only two of us," their step-mother said, "what little food we have would go further. If there were only two of us, we could leave this miserable hovel and seek work elsewhere."

"What work would there be for a poor woodcutter," the children's father sighed, "far from the trees he knows?"

"You would learn to turn your hand to something else," said his wife. "Hunger is a good teacher. Tomorrow we must take Hansel and Gretel to the heart of the forest. They will play in the clearing while we work. We will leave them there when we come home, and what will happen, will happen."

"No, no, woman," cried the woodcutter. "Bears and wolves will tear them to pieces. How can I do this to my children whom I love so much?"

"Would it be better," said his wife, "if they died more slowly from starvation? There is hardly a crust left in the house."

Upstairs, Gretel began to weep.

Hansel whispered, "Gretel, do not cry. I know what has to be done."

When their father and step-mother were asleep, Hansel went downstairs and opened the front door. Every small stone lying on the ground glowed white in the moonlight. Hansel filled his pockets with them, and returned to the house and to his bed.

Next day, the woodcutter said, "We will be working in a different part of the forest today. You may come with us and wait in the clearing until we have finished."

As they walked, the trees grew taller and taller and closer and closer together. When she saw how Hansel turned again and again to look back at the path they were following, his step-mother said, "What's the matter? Why are you looking back? Surely you know where you have come from, silly boy!"

"Yes," said Hansel, "only I thought I saw my white cat sitting on the windowsill as we left, and I was waving goodbye."

They reached the clearing. The woodcutter lit a fire and his wife gave each of the children a thick slice of bread.

"Stay here," she said, "until we come back."

When the woodcutter and his wife had gone, Hansel and Gretel sat beside the fire. They could hear the sound of the axe striking at the wood coming from far away. The fire burned low, and the children ate their bread. Gretel slept a little, and Hansel watched over her. By the time she woke up, twilight had crept into the forest.

"They will not come for us," said Hansel. "They have left us here to be eaten by wolves and bears."

"But I can still hear Father's axe striking the wood. Listen!" said Gretel.

"While you were asleep, I walked among the trees. I found a log tied to a small branch. Every time the wind moves it, it knocks against the trunk of an oak. They have tricked us into waiting, but soon we will find our way home again."

After the moon had risen, Hansel and Gretel set off down the path that they had taken that morning.

"Can you see that small white stone, sister, glowing in the moonlight?"

"Yes, Hansel, and another one there . . . and there."

"I dropped them, one by one, on our journey this morning," said Hansel, "and now they will lead us to the door of our cottage."

The children walked all night, stepping from white stone to white stone, and as the sun came up, they knocked on the door of their own house.

"Oh, my beloved children," said the woodcutter, weeping. "I thought you were lost for ever."

"I hope," said their step-mother, unsmiling, "that you are not expecting a hearty breakfast, for a thin gruel is all we have."

"We are in our own home again," said Gretel. "The food doesn't matter."

"You will change your tune," said her step-mother, " after a few days with nothing at all to eat."

That night, the children listened once again to the voices from the room below.

"In a week or so," said their step-mother, "we will be four skeletons sitting at the table. Let us go even deeper into the forest. This time they will not find their way back."

Hansel said, "I will go down and pick up stones again. I shall need even more than I had before."

When all was quiet, he tiptoed downstairs, but the front door of the cottage was locked. He stared out of the window and trembled. How would he make his way now? He hid his fears from Gretel, saying only, "Do not worry, sister. There will be other ways of finding the path."

Next morning, their step-mother gave them each a thick slice of bread.

"This must last you till nightfall, children," she said. "Look after it."

Gretel put her slice into her apron pocket, but Hansel rubbed his portion into a million crumbs. These he scattered along the path as they walked, rejoicing that now their way was marked again.

"Why do you turn back so often, Hansel?" his step-mother asked him.

"My little white cat is up on the roof," said Hansel, "and I am waving it goodbye."

The children followed their father and step-mother into the very heart of the forest. In a small clearing, the woodcutter built a fire, and once again set off with his wife, leaving the children alone. When Hansel told her what he had done with his slice of bread, Gretel said, "We will share my slice, and wait until the moon rises."

Later, the moon sailed through the dark sky, and the children began to look for crumbs along the path.

"I cannot see them," said Hansel. And Gretel cried, "But alas, the birds that fly in these branches must have seen them and eaten them long ago. Why did we not think more carefully?"

"Dry your tears, Gretel," said Hansel, "and come with me. We must walk and see where the path leads us, for if we stay here, surely bears and wolves will tear us to pieces."

The children walked. They walked through the night. Night became day and all through the day they went on walking, faint with hunger and fearful of every sound. Branches tore at their clothes; the soles of their shoes were worn so thin that every stone bruised their feet.

"Let us rest, Hansel," said Gretel, "just for a moment."

The children sat down in the shade of a tree.

"Look at that pretty bird," Hansel said. "Listen to its song."

"I think," said Gretel, "that it is talking to us. I think it wants to show us the way."

"Let us go where it leads us, then," said Hansel, jumping to his feet. The white bird flew off the branch, and fluttered through the trees, and the children followed.

"Look!" said Gretel, after some hours had passed. "I knew the bird would bring us good luck. Have you ever seen such a house, Hansel?"

Brother and sister stood open-mouthed in the clearing to which they had come, gazing at a house that belonged in dreams. A fragrance of cinnamon hung in the air, for the walls of this small cottage were made of freshly-baked biscuit. The roof was cut from slabs of cake heavy with fruit and nuts, and the windows were clear spun-sugar that dazzled the children, glittering in the last rays of the sun and shining into their eyes.

"Who lives here?" said Gretel. "Go to the door, Hansel, and see if anyone is at home."

As her brother knocked, Gretel began to lick the windows and nibble the window-ledges. Never in her life before had she tasted anything quite so delicious.

The door opened suddenly and an old woman stepped out. She smiled at Hansel and Gretel.

"Welcome, welcome to my house, my little darlings! I have been longing and longing for your visit. The meal has been prepared and your bedroom is ready."

Hansel and Gretel rejoiced at their good fortune. The old woman showed them soft beds made up with sheets that smelled of lavender. After their bath, they ate a meal of thick soup, followed by golden pancakes stuffed with apples.

"I have my own oven," said the old woman. "Come, I will show it to you."

In the kitchen stood something like a huge black cupboard. From deep within it came a sound like roaring.

"Those are the flames, my little ducklings," said the old woman. "The flames that roast. I shall open the door and you can see."

Gretel turned away. The fires in the oven's black heart reminded her of pictures she had seen of Hell.

"I think," she said later to her brother as they lay between the cool white sheets, "that this old woman may be a witch, Hansel."

"Why do you say so, sister, when she has taken us in and fed us so well?"

"She has red eyes. That is a sure sign, they say."

"Red or not," said Hansel, "they are very weak. She peers at everything as though she can hardly see it."

The next day, the old woman asked Hansel to come and help her fetch a chicken from the poultry-cage to roast for supper. Hansel followed her.

"This cage is empty," he told the old woman.

"It was empty," said she, pushing Hansel as hard as she could, "but now you are in it, and I shall keep you here until you are ready for the roasting." She laughed, and the sound made Hansel shiver. "I have waited years," she whispered. "You may imagine how hungry I am, my little dumpling!"

From that moment on, everything changed. Gretel became a servant to the old woman, fetching and carrying and sweeping and scrubbing all day long. She took delicious meals to Hansel in the cage, and he shared them with her. If it had not been for her brother's kindness, Gretel would have starved on what the old woman, who was certainly a witch, provided for her.

Every third day, Hansel was inspected to see if he was plump enough for roasting, and each time the witch approached his cage, he held out a chicken-bone for her to feel. Because her eyesight was so weak, she thought the bone was Hansel's finger, and her anger swelled and grew.

"I thought you would grow fat," she growled, "but you are skinnier than ever. Never mind, I can wait no longer. You will be roasted tomorrow."

The next morning, the witch took Gretel into the kitchen.

"We will make the bread first, girl," she told her. "I have prepared the dough. Open the door and put the loaves in."

"I have forgotten how to slide the loaves into the oven," Gretel said. "Show me how and I will do it."

"Silly goose," said the witch. "Surely you have seen me baking often and often. I open the oven door so, and I push the tray as far as I can into the oven . . . so . . ."

She leaned in towards the flames. Gretel grabbed her feet and pushed with every drop of strength left in her body. In the time it takes to blink, the witch fell headlong into the oven. Gretel slammed the black door shut and fled from the room. She took a bunch of keys from a hook beside the door and ran to let Hansel out of his cage.

"I have closed the oven door on her," Gretel told her brother. "She will not trouble us again."

She unlocked the cage and Hansel stepped out.

"Quick, sister," he said. "We must take some food from the witch's kitchen for our journey and flee this evil place."

Before they left, the children opened the trunk which stood in a shadowy corner of the cottage. In it were pearls, and rubies like ripe cherries, and enough gold coins to fill a thousand purses.

"The witch is dead," said Hansel. "She has no need of this treasure now. Let us take as much as we can."

Gretel filled her apron pockets with gemstones and Hansel made a bundle out of rags and tied up as much gold as he could.

"Which way shall we go?" Gretel asked as they came once more into the forest.

"We shall go where Fortune takes us," Hansel answered.

Just before nightfall, the children reached a lake.

"This lake is wide, and deep too, for all we know," said Hansel. "How will we cross to the other side? We cannot swim."

Just at that moment, a white swan came out of the reeds on the riverbank, and spoke to the children:

"Trust me, children; I will take
each of you across this lake."

Gretel went first. She sat on the swan's back, between its white wings, and together they skimmed across the water to the far bank. There Gretel waited while the enchanted bird returned for her brother.

"Thank you, beautiful creature!" the children cried as the swan went back to the reeds. "Thank you with all our hearts."

Hansel and Gretel went on walking. They walked for many hours, until Gretel said, "Brother, look through those branches. Do you see that red roof in the distance?"

"Yes," said Hansel, "and I can see my white cat sitting on the roof waiting to welcome me. That is our house, Gretel. We have come home."

The children began to weep tears of pure joy. Their father, full of bitter remorse for his own wickedness, greeted them with hugs and kisses. Their step-mother had died only a week before.

"I should never have listened to her," said the children's father. "How can you ever forgive me?"

"We forgive you," said Gretel. And Hansel said, "See what we have brought you!" He showed his father the witch's treasure. "Hunger will never again look in at our window."

And Hunger never did. Hansel and Gretel and their father lived out the rest of their days in great prosperity and good health.

THE TINDERBOX

For many years, a terrible war had raged in the land, but now it was over. A soldier who had been paid good money by the King while he was fighting, suddenly found himself with not a penny piece to call his own. His only possessions were the clothes he stood up in, his sword, and the knapsack he carried on his back. He was walking along a quiet road one morning when he met an old woman.

"Good morning, soldier," she cried when she saw him. "You are sent to help me, I can see that. And I can see that you would not say no to the offer of as many gold coins as you can carry away with you."

The soldier looked closely at the old woman, and shivered. Her teeth were like tombstones, her skin like leather and her hands like the claws of an ancient lizard. Perhaps she was a witch. Perhaps she would change him into a worm if he refused her, so he said, "I'm happy to help you, madam. Only show me where the gold may be found."

"The gold will be your reward for bringing me back my old tinderbox. This lies within the hollow trunk of that tree over there. I shall tie a rope around your waist, and let you down into the tree, and when you have found the tinderbox, you must call up to me and I shall pull you out."

"Very well," said the soldier, "but what of the gold?"

"Come here to me," said the old woman, "and I will whisper in your ear exactly what you must do to find it."

The soldier put his ear to the crone's shrivelled lips, and, shuddering, he listened carefully to every word she uttered. Then she took off her apron.

"You will need this," she said, "if you are to come back alive."

Down and down into the heart of the tree went the soldier, with the old woman's rope tied round his waist. He came to rest at the bottom and saw, stretching before him, a corridor lit by a thousand lamps.

"She said it would be so," he murmured and walked towards a door he could see in the distance. This he opened and found himself in a room which had nothing in it but a chest, and on top of the chest sat a dog with eyes as big as saucers. This creature growled horribly at the soldier, and bared its fearsome fangs.

"You cannot frighten me, sir," said the soldier, "for she said it would be so. I am to spread her apron out thus and you, sir, are to sit on it while I help myself to whatever I may find."

The soldier placed the dog upon the apron, and opened the chest.

"Copper coins," he said to himself. "Well, I am in need of gold, but what if I never reach it? Copper is better than nothing." He filled his pockets with the money, closed the chest and put the dog back exactly as he had found him. He then picked up the old woman's apron and went through the door. The corridor had vanished, and the soldier found himself in a larger room, which had another chest in it and another dog.

"You cannot frighten me, sir," said the soldier, "for she said it would be so." The dog stared about him with eyes the size of soup plates, and let its tongue loll out between its enormous jaws.

The soldier spread the apron and placed the dog upon it, groaning a little under the animal's weight. Then he opened the chest.

"Silver coins this time," he shouted, and tossed every bit of copper out on to the floor, filling his pockets and knapsack with the new treasure.

"Back to your chest you go, sir," he said to the dog, "and I shall open the door once more."

This time the soldier found himself in a room as high and wide as a cathedral nave. The chest was larger than any he had ever seen before, and the dog that sat upon it was a monster from the worst of his dreams, with eyes the size of mill-wheels.

"I shall not be frightened," the soldier said to himself, "for she said it would be so."

He struggled and heaved and strained every muscle in his body until at last the fiendish cur was seated on the apron and the chest lay ready to be opened.

"Gold," the soldier breathed, unable to believe his luck. He threw every silver coin to the ground and filled his pockets, his knapsack and his boots with as much treasure as he could carry.

"It has all happened as the old woman said," he thought. "She is surely a witch."

This time, when he stepped out of the room, he found himself once more in the long corridor.

"Pull me up now, old woman," he called. "I have my gold."

"But where is my tinderbox?" came an answering voice from somewhere far away.

"Why, I forgot it altogether," the soldier laughed. "Wait but one moment and I shall return and fetch it." The tinderbox was in the chest full of gold coins, and the soldier seized it and pulled on the rope to show that he was ready.

When she saw him come out of the tree, the old woman smiled. "Give me my tinderbox, young man," she said.

And the soldier answered, "Only when you have told me why it is so important to you."

"That I shall never tell you," said the old woman, and she began to cackle dreadfully.

"If you do not tell me," said the soldier, "I shall run you through with my sword."

The crone refused to say another word, and the soldier, in a fury at her stubbornness, killed her and left her lying under the tree. He spread out her apron and poured out on to it every gold coin he had taken. Then he tossed the tinderbox on top of all the money, tied the corners of the apron together, and set out for the city.

The soldier was now a wealthy man. He bought a fine house and filled it with rich ornaments. He bought new clothes. Everyone became his friend, and the rooms of his house were filled with his feasting and carousing companions.

This life of pleasure continued for a while, but when the last gold coin was spent, the soldier was forced to sell everything he owned. The friends who had been so affectionate while he was rich, disappeared as though they had never existed, and after some months the soldier found himself living in a chilly attic room with a leaky roof. Once again, all he possessed were the clothes he stood up in, his sword and his knapsack.

One night, he put his hand into the knapsack, thinking that perhaps he might have left a single gold coin there by mistake, and his fingers touched the old woman's tinderbox.

"Why," he cried, "again I have forgotten all about you! You may not be treasure, but at least now I may burn a candle for a while."

He struck the flint, a yellow light flared in the room, and there before him was the dog with eyes as big as saucers.

"Do not fear me, Master," said the dog, "for I come to grant your dearest wish."

The soldier thought, "This is a dream. Perhaps I have a fever. Nevertheless, I shall make a wish."

"Money," he said to the dog. "I need all the money I had before, and I need it to last a good while longer."

The soldier's wish was granted instantly. Soon he was back in his fine house, dressed in the best clothes, and all his old friends had returned as well. Once more, he was a happy man.

One evening, the talk turned to the Princess. No one had ever seen her, but the story was that she was very beautiful. The King and Queen had kept her locked in a palace carved from ivory since her birth, because

a fortune-teller once said that she would marry a commoner.

"I should dearly love to see her," said the soldier when his friends had gone home, and he took out the tinderbox and struck it twice. A yellow light flared and the dog with eyes as big as soup plates sat before him.

"What does my master wish?" said this creature.

"I wish to see the Princess," the soldier answered. "Bring her to me."

"I obey you, my master," said the dog, "and I shall fetch her here at once."

The Princess leaned against her pillows and said to her mother, "You cannot imagine what a strange dream I had. I dreamed that I rode on the back of an enormous dog to a fine house in the city. There I met a soldier who kissed my hand and told me I was to be his bride. He was very handsome, Mother. Imagine if I should meet such a man when I was awake."

The Queen told the King and together they decided that not the smallest risk should be taken. The Princess's nurse was to keep watch all night and report to them the next day.

That night, once again, the soldier struck the tinderbox twice and bade the dog with eyes like soup plates to bring the Princess to his house.

The dog did as he was told. He noticed that the Princess's nurse was following them through the dark streets; he saw the woman chalk a mark on the door of the soldier's house and outwitted her by marking every door in the street. When the King and Queen came looking for the house the following day, they would be quite unable to find it.

On the third night, the soldier struck the tinderbox three times, a yellow light flared, and the dog with eyes like mill-wheels appeared. He was sent at once to fetch the Princess. This time the Queen had tied a bag of flour to her daughter's girdle, and she had cut a tiny hole in the fabric. As the huge dog ran through the streets with the Princess on his back, a trail of flour showed where they were bound. The very next day, the King's guard seized the soldier and locked him in a prison cell.

"You will be hanged at dawn tomorrow," said the King, "for kidnapping a Royal Princess and bringing her to your house."

The soldier looked out of the cell window. He called out to a small boy, playing in the street outside the prison.

"Go to my lodging, young fellow," he said, "and bring me the tinderbox you find there. If you do this for me, you may help yourself to as much money as you can find in my house."

The boy flew to the soldier's house, and was back within the hour. He threw the tinderbox up to the soldier's window and wished him well.

The next day at dawn, the soldier was brought to the scaffold. The King and Queen were there, together with rows and rows of judges and legal gentlemen of every shape and size. A large crowd had gathered.

The soldier addressed the King, saying, "Will you grant a condemned man a last request? I wish to smoke a pipe of tobacco before the hangman does his work."

"I can see no objection to that," said the King, and immediately a pipe full of tobacco was put into the soldier's hand. He took the tinderbox from his pocket, and struck it three times. A yellow light flared, and at once the dog with eyes like mill-wheels appeared, with the two smaller dogs at his heels.

"We are come to do your bidding, Master," they said, and the soldier nodded.

"Save me from the gallows," he said, "and let my enemies be scattered."

The dogs set about the King and Queen and all the judges, tossing them into the air like so many rag-dolls.

"You must be our King," the crowd shouted.

So the soldier married the Princess, and the three dogs of the tinderbox ensured that they were happy and prosperous to the end of their days.

RAPUNZEL

On a summer day, in a faraway country, a young woman stood at her window. She was awaiting the coming of her first child, which would be born when the first snow fell.

"How lovely the enchanted garden is!" she sighed.

"It is not our garden," said her husband.

"I have seen the Lady who owns it," said the woman. "People say she is a sorceress, but I believe they are envious of the beauty of her garden."

She smiled at her husband.

"My mother told me that women who are with child long for certain foods, and now I see she was right. I crave a salad made from rampion, and there is some growing in the garden. Will you go and pick it for me?

"I dare not," her husband said.

The woman began to weep.

"If you do not fetch me some rampion, I shall die, and you will be a grieving widower."

Her husband sighed. "I shall climb into the garden tonight, and bring back what you long for."

The clock had just struck midnight as the young man climbed the wall and jumped into the garden. Silently he made his way along the paths to the corner where the rampion grew. As he knelt down to pull it from the earth, he heard a voice saying, "You are a brave man." Looking up in terror he saw a tall woman standing beside him.

"Be merciful, my lady. I am no thief. My wife and I expect a baby at the turn of the year, and she craves a salad made from rampion. If she does not have it, she says, she will pine and die."

The Lady considered her reply. Finally she said, "You may take the rampion, but I will expect payment."

"Oh, thank you . . . I will give you anything."

"Anything?" said the Lady.

The young man said, "There is nothing I would not do for my wife."

"Take the rampion," said the Lady. "When the first snow falls, I shall return for my payment."

"But what is the payment?"

The Lady laughed and her laugh was like the thin cry of a night-bird. "What I want is your child, when that child is born."

*

Suns rose and set; moons waxed and waned and a baby girl was born on the longest night of the year. Outside, the whole world was white. In the nursery a fire burned, but the young woman and her husband sitting beside it were cold with misery.

When the Lady came to collect the child, nothing was said at first. The baby was lifted from her cradle and wrapped in a shawl of fine wool. At the threshold, the Lady turned and spoke.

"This child will be treasured," she said. "I will keep her safe from the world. And I shall call her Rapunzel, which is the country name for rampion."

After the Lady and the baby had gone, the woman said, "We must leave this place, for I could not bear to see the child playing in the garden and know she can never be ours."

The very next day, the couple left their house, and were never seen again.

Suns rose and set; moons waxed and waned. No scissors ever came near Rapunzel's hair, and it grew longer and longer and shone like golden silk. Rapunzel knew that the person who looked after her was not the one who had given birth to her, but she called the Lady "Mother" just the same. As she often said, "I love you and you look after me, and have done since I was a tiny baby."

"You are a baby no longer," said the Lady. "You have reached the age of twelve, and I must now hide you even more secretly."

"Braid my hair, then, Mother, and tie it with a scarlet ribbon, and I will follow wherever you may lead me."

The very next day, Rapunzel and the Lady set out for the forest.

"Where are you taking me, Mother?" Rapunzel asked. "What will I find there?"

"I am taking you to the Tower," said the Lady, "and there you will live, alone."

"Alone?" whispered Rapunzel. "What of you, Mother? Where will you be?"

"I shall be watching over you. You will never know. I could be a bird, or a blowing leaf."

"Will I never see you?" Rapunzel asked. "I shall be so lonely."

"Every morning," said the Lady, "I shall visit you. I will stand at the foot of the Tower, and you will let down your plaited hair from the high window. I will climb up the rope of your hair, and bring you food and drink and my company for an hour, but no longer."

"Why," asked Rapunzel, "could you not climb the stairs to my room?"

"You will see, my dear."

They came at last to the Tower. The door sprang open, and Rapunzel followed the Lady up a spiral staircase. The room at the top of the Tower had everything in it that a person could wish for.

"You will be happy here," the Lady said. "See, this is the window. Before you let your braid down to me, twist it around this iron catch. Then you will hardly feel my weight pulling on your hair."

Rapunzel said, "Any pain I feel will not be in my hair, Mother, but in my heart. I would be so much happier if you were here with me."

The Lady said, "After I leave, there will be no stairs. They will vanish, and so will the door. But listen for my voice and remember that I care only for your happiness."

Rapunzel watched as the one she thought of as her mother began to make her way down the stairs. As she trod on each step, it seemed to melt, and a stream of liquid stone flowed silently through the Tower, filling it and filling it until it was solid all the way through. "There is no one," thought Rapunzel, "to hear me cry."

She looked out of the window. Far below her she could see something that might have been the Lady's cloak moving like swift wings through the forest. Rapunzel looked at her own face in the mirror.

"I must become accustomed to my own company," she said to her reflection, "or I shall surely perish."

Suns rose and set; moons waxed and waned; the years turned and Rapunzel grew into a young woman. A hedge of thorn-bushes had sprung up all around the Tower, and none but the Lady ever came near it, until one day, a prince who was riding in the forest chanced to hear the Lady calling:

> *"Rapunzel fair,*
> *let down your hair.*
> *Let down the gold rope*
> *of your hair."*

He followed the sound through the trees and at last he saw a beautiful young woman looking out of a high window, and an older woman climbing up to the window using a thickly-braided plait of hair as her rope.

"This must be an enchanted Tower," said the prince to himself, "for it has no door. But I have seen the face of a young woman at the window, and I will not rest until I speak to her."

He waited until the Lady had climbed down the golden rope and vanished between the trees, and then he came to the foot of the Tower and called:

"Let down the gold rope
of your hair.
Rapunzel fair,
let down your hair."

The words flew up to Rapunzel in her room.

"It must be my mother," she thought, "although she does not sound like herself and she has never come to me at dusk before."

At once, she tied her hair to the iron catch and threw her plait out of the window. A few moments later, a person such as she had never seen in her life climbed into the room.

"Oh!" Rapunzel fell back in terror. "Who are you? You are not my mother. Will you harm me? Please, I beg you, do not come near me."

"I would never harm you," said the prince. "My name is Marius, and I am the son of a king. All I want is to speak to you, and gaze at your beauty."

Rapunzel looked into the young man's grey eyes and listened to his voice and knew she had nothing to fear.

"I have longed for someone to talk to," she said. "I have never spoken to anyone but my mother. Tell me of the world beyond my Tower."

Marius told her of the world. Every day at dusk he climbed up to her room. He grew to love Rapunzel, and she loved him. Soon, she spent every day waiting for the moment when she would see him, and parting from him became an agonizing sorrow for her.

One night, Marius said, "We do not have to part. I can take you from this Tower to my father's kingdom. You will be my wife and we shall be happy for ever."

So Rapunzel devised a plan.

"Bring me skeins of the strongest thread," she said, "and I will fashion a ladder. When it is long enough, I shall fasten it to the iron catch and climb down. I want to leave the Tower. I have been too much on my own. I shall be your wife and live in your kingdom."

Suns rose and set; moons waxed and waned and every day Rapunzel added another foot to the ladder she was making.

All would have been well, if she had guarded her tongue more carefully, but her thoughts were so full of Marius that by chance one day she said to the Lady, "Is it not astonishing that Marius for all his height does not weigh on my hair as heavily as you do?"

As she spoke the words, Rapunzel saw a terrible change come over the one she called her mother. Her face darkened, her eyes grew red with the fires of rage and she trembled so dreadfully that it seemed to Rapunzel the whole Tower rocked on its foundations. At first, the Lady uttered not a single word. She drew a pair of silver shears from an inner pocket and severed Rapunzel's plait from her head with a hideous crunching of metal. Then she spoke.

"You will come with me," she said.

"But how," Rapunzel cried, "when there are no stairs?"

"There are stairs," said the Lady, "whenever I need them. Follow me."

Round and round and down and down they went, and at last they left the Tower.

"Where are you taking me?" wept Rapunzel. "I have nothing with me but the clothes I am wearing."

They walked in silence for an hour and then for another. The forest ended and before them stretched a desert. Crested waves and mountain peaks of sand filled the landscape, with no rock or tree or patch of shade from one end of the horizon to the other.

"You are truly alone now," said the Lady. "Whatever will happen to you, will happen." With these words, she turned and Rapunzel watched her growing smaller and smaller as she walked away, until she could no longer be seen.

"Oh, Marius!" Rapunzel called into the empty sky. "What will she do to you? How will I bear this fate?" Her voice echoed in the wilderness and no one answered.

That evening, Marius approached the Tower with joy in his heart. The ladder was long enough, and he and Rapunzel could flee at last. His voice rang out:

"Let down your hair,
Rapunzel fair.
Let down the gold rope
of your hair."

The plait fell from the window. "This is the last time," Marius thought. "I shall never do this again."

The Lady was waiting for him. She had tied Rapunzel's severed plait to the iron catch, and as he stepped into the room, she said, "You are surprised to see me. You were expecting Rapunzel."

Marius cried, "What have you done? Where have you taken her? How will I ever find her?"

The Lady laughed and her laughter echoed round the room like the thin cry of a night bird.

"You will never find her. She has been banished and she will surely die."

"Then you will die with her!" said Marius, and he flung himself at the

Lady. She writhed and turned in his grasp, like some dark snake, and he felt the strength of her fury, and found himself pushed towards the open window.

"I cannot die," shrieked the Lady, "but you – you are a trespasser and a thief of love and you deserve to lose your life."

The Lady twisted out of Marius's arms and touched his neck with one long finger. The king's son flinched, for it was as though a blazing torch had been held to his throat. The pain caused him to stagger backwards and he lost his footing.

"Drop!" cried the Lady. "Plummet to your doom!" And Marius fell, down and down to the base of the Tower. He should have died, but the bushes broke his fall. When he struggled to his feet, he rejoiced to find himself alive, but his eyes had been pierced by thorns and tears of blood streamed down his cheeks.

"Foul enchantress!" he called up to the window. "I may be blind, but I am alive. I will seek Rapunzel until my last day on this earth, and I will find her."

Suns rose and set; moons waxed and waned; the years turned and Marius wandered the world in search of Rapunzel.

One day, the prince heard a song, blown on a passing wind. He recognized Rapunzel's voice and followed it.

"Rapunzel!" he cried. "Are you there? Is it you? Speak to me. Tell me where you are."

"Marius!" Rapunzel ran to his side and covered his face with kisses. "You have found us. I knew you would come. Oh, this is a happy day!"

Her tears of joy fell on to Marius's face, and soon he realized that his eyes were healed and he could see again. What he saw filled his heart with pleasure. Rapunzel stood before him, and sitting in the shade of a tree were two small children.

"These twins," said Rapunzel, "were born to me in the desert. And see, I watered the wilderness with so many tears that it will soon be green again."

"Come," said Marius, taking his children by the hand, "we will find the way to my father's kingdom."

Rapunzel and Marius left the desert for ever, and they and their children lived the rest of their lives in the most perfect happiness.

VIPERS AND PEARLS

❧

There was once a woman who had two daughters. When the first child was born, she named her Ruby and the second she called Rose. Ruby grew up to resemble her mother, while Rose took after her father in every way.

Ruby and Rose were still very young when their father died. Their mother favoured her elder daughter, and poor Rose was neglected. She was made to do much of the hard scrubbing and daily cooking for the three of them, while Ruby arranged and rearranged her hair in front of the mirror, and discussed with her mother how best she might find a wealthy and handsome husband.

"Only a prince," said the Widow, "would be good enough for you, my jewel and treasure."

"But how," said Ruby, "will I ever meet a prince while we live in this dingy little cottage? Why, we have to walk two miles to bring water from the well – which reminds me: Rose, it is nearly time. You should set out now, I think, if I am to wash my hands before supper."

Rose took up a bucket and left the cottage. When she came to the well, she noticed an old woman leaning against it, looking as though she would faint from hunger and thirst.

"Can I help you, Old Mother?" asked Rose, for she was as kind as she was pretty, and her heart ached to see the old woman's torn clothes and toothless, shrivelled face.

"A drink from the well would be Paradise," said the old woman. "But I have no bucket."

"I have a bucket," said Rose, "and you may drink your fill, and wash yourself, too, if that would please you."

Rose let the bucket down into the well, and drew out the clear water. The old woman drank and drank and then dipped her face and hands into the bucket.

"Is there anything else I can do for you," Rose asked, "before I bring up a bucket of water to take home?"

"You have done more than you know," said the old woman. "And you shall be rewarded for it. I am no ordinary person, and you shall see the proof of it when you return to your home, for every syllable that falls from your mouth will turn into a gemstone."

When Rose arrived at the cottage, Ruby and the Widow were furious.

"You are late with the water!" they cried. "How are we supposed to prepare ourselves for supper? And there is still the table to be laid, and the soup to be heated."

Rose said, "I shall do all that at once. I am sorry I am late, only I met an old woman near the well and gave her some water."

Ruby and the Widow shrank back against the dresser in amazement, for as Rose spoke, pearls and diamonds fell from her mouth and rolled and bounced about on the floor.

"The old woman said this would happen," Rose said, and more pearls sprang from her lips, followed by diamonds that caught the light and glittered, dazzling the Widow and Ruby until they could scarcely see.

"She must have been a Fairy in disguise," the Widow said. "Tell me exactly what happened; exactly what you said to her and she said to you."

As Rose spoke, so many gemstones fell from her mouth that small heaps of them began to form here and there on the floor.

"Why should Rose have such treasures," the Widow whined, "when her sister cannot? A prince would surely come and marry you, Ruby, if he knew you had such magical powers. Tomorrow morning you must go to the well. You must do just what Rose did, and see if the Fairy will bless you in the same way."

The next morning, Ruby began grumbling at dawn. "Why should I have to lower myself in this fashion," she asked, "going to the well, like an ordinary person and speaking to grubby old women who may or may not be fairies. After all, we only have Rose's word for it. Maybe she is lying. Maybe a magical bird flew by, or maybe the well-water itself is enchanted. I want nothing to do with smelly old women in rags."

"You will go," said the Widow, "and what is more, you will be as polite as possible. Only think how enormously wealthy we shall be!"

Ruby set off. When she reached the well, there was no one there at all. "I daresay," said Ruby to herself, "I shall now have to wait here for the crone to appear."

At that moment, a finely-dressed Lady came up to her. It was the same Fairy who had spoken to Rose, but in a disguise as different from the first as mud is from water.

"Will you lend me your bucket, pretty maid?" said the Lady. "I have been walking and walking in the heat and a drink would cool me."

"I don't see," said Ruby, "why people cannot bring their own buckets to the well, but must forever be borrowing from others. Still, I suppose I shall have to lend it to you." She thrust the bucket roughly into the Lady's hand. There was a scowl on her face, and she did not so much as glance at her grandly-dressed companion. She was wondering where the old woman was: the giver of gifts.

"Here is your bucket," said the Lady.

"You have not exactly hurried, have you?" said Ruby. "I must go home now. I hate waiting for anything and I shall certainly waste no more time idling beside this well. Perhaps I shall reap my reward for letting *you* borrow my bucket."

"Assuredly," said the Lady. "Your reward will be swift and just."

When Ruby arrived at the cottage, her mother was peering anxiously out of the door.

"Come in, come in, child, and tell me everything that you did at the well."

"Nothing happened," said Ruby, and as she opened her mouth, a mass of slithering vipers and brown toads fell from her lips and wriggled and hopped all over the floor. "The old lady never appeared. It was doubtless one of Rose's lies."

The Widow covered her face with her apron and moaned. Rose turned pale and jumped on to a chair.

"It is her fault!" Ruby shrieked. She pointed at her sister, and more slimy toads and spotted vipers writhed down from between her teeth and hid among her skirts. "She has bewitched me. Get rid of her, Mother. Put her out of doors."

Together, Ruby and the Widow started to hit poor Rose, and push her, until she was outside the cottage. Then they locked the door against her, and shouted through the keyhole, "Go away from here. Never come back. You are not the Rose who was our flesh and blood, but a wicked enchantress."

Rose walked away from the cottage and into the forest. She wept to think of her loneliness and misery. Suddenly, she heard the sound of hooves drumming on the earth and a young man appeared, riding a white horse. Rose made as though to hide behind one of the trees, and the young man called out to her, "Stay, do not flee. I am a Prince, and will not harm you. Only tell me the way to the nearest town, for I am lost in this forest."

Rose looked at the Prince, and saw that he was the handsomest young man she had ever seen. The Prince looked at Rose, and thought, "This is the young woman who must be my bride."

Rose said, "The town lies an hour's ride to the west." As she spoke, pearls and diamonds poured from her mouth, and in amongst the jewels, there were flowers also: pink rosebuds and white lilies and scarlet camellias. The ground at Rose's feet was carpeted with fragrant blooms and precious gems.

The Prince said, "Come with me to the town, and be my bride, and one day we will rule the kingdom together."

He lifted Rose on to his horse, and they rode away to the west.

As for Ruby, she was banished from her home. Her mother could no longer

endure the foul creatures that rolled off her tongue, and so she put her elder daughter to live in a distant cave. Twice a day, she took her a meal, and then returned to the empty cottage.

The Widow never learned of Rose's good fortune. She heard from a passing pedlar that the Prince was to wed, but she said to herself, "Such things do not concern me any longer. I shan't give the matter another thought."

BLUEBEARD

"Everything I have," said Bluebeard to his Bride, "is yours."

The young woman considered the palace which was now her home. Its towers rose into the clouds and its gardens stretched to the sea. She thought of the fine tapestries lining long corridors; the cabinets crowded with the most delicate porcelain dishes; the carpets from Persia and the gold lamps that hung from the high ceilings, and she knew that her husband was a rich man.

"He is far wealthier," the Bride thought, "than even my mother imagined when she begged me to marry him." The Bride remembered her mother's words. "Do not be frightened, my dear. It is true that he is old and has been married before, but old men are indulgent. You will want for nothing."

It was not her husband's age that had made the young woman hesitate, but he was a man whose appearance filled her heart with dread. He was immensely tall, with a pale face and eyes set in sockets as dark as caves. His beard was of a blue as deep as oceans and flowed from his chin to his waist like a tumbling waterfall of hair.

But he had dazzled her with gifts and soothed her with kind words. He promised that she could fill the palace and the terraced gardens with parties of her young friends, who were all welcome to enjoy themselves at his expense. He even permitted Anne, the Bride's sister, to move into an apartment in the East Wing.

So the couple were married, and their life together began.

One day, Bluebeard came to his Bride and said, "I have to go on a journey, my dear, to see to some business matters in the city. I will be away several weeks, and while I am gone, you are in charge of my palace, and of everything I own. Here are the keys. You may make what use of them you will, but there is one room at the end of the North Corridor which is locked and must remain so. I warn you: on no account use the smallest silver key which unlocks it if you value your life."

After Bluebeard rode away, the Bride looked carefully at the smallest silver key. Whatever she tried to do and wherever she went, thoughts of the locked door at the end of the North Corridor nagged at her and filled her head, until she had nothing in her mind at all but a sharp longing to see what her husband was so careful to hide away.

"I will be discovered and his anger will be terrible," she said to herself. But then she said, "Why should I be discovered? I have the smallest silver key. I will unlock the door and only peep into the room. Then I will lock the door again, and Bluebeard will never, ever know, for surely, I shall say nothing."

Next day, she waited until her sister and all the servants were busy, and then she tiptoed down the North Corridor. In her hand she held the smallest silver key. She had removed it from the ring which held all the others, in case the rattling should wake one of the footmen.

She hesitated for a moment in front of the black door. "Perhaps," she thought, "I should go back to my bed . . . but how will I rest if I do not discover what is hidden?" Her curiosity was stronger than her fear and she turned the key in the lock.

The door opened quite silently. She took the smallest silver key out of the keyhole and held it as she stepped into the room. The floor was sticky with something which glistened nearly black in the light from the window. Could it be blood?

Alas! It was. The entire chamber was filled with the mortal remains of Bluebeard's previous wives!

In her terror, the Bride dropped the smallest silver key on the floor, and when she picked it up, it was so slippery that she could hardly grasp it. The key was no longer silver, but crimson with blood, and even though the Bride wiped it and wiped it on her skirt, crimson it remained as she fled from the room and locked the black door with trembling fingers.

She flew to her room and lay there, shivering. What if Bluebeard returned and found the key missing from the ring? She must clean it and put it back with the rest.

That night, the Bride washed the key, again and again. She scrubbed and scrubbed and thought at first that the stain had gone, but when she turned the key over, there it still was on the other side, as red as an open wound.

The next evening, standing in the garden at twilight, the Bride thought, "I will bury the key, but then what will I say to my husband when he asks me where it is?" She looked towards the sea. "Thank goodness," she said to herself at last, "that Bluebeard is not returning for some weeks. In that time, I will decide what must be done."

She made her way back to the palace, and the first person she saw was Bluebeard.

"You are surprised to see me, my dear," he said. "I finished my business earlier than I had planned and rode home as quickly as I could to be with you, my Bride."

"That is kind of you," said the Bride. "I am delighted to see you." She smiled and smiled. Her whole body grew cold with fear. She knew that it would not be long before Bluebeard asked for his keys. She would do all that was in her power to make her husband happy. Perhaps she could make him so happy that he would forget about keys for a little while.

The couple dined from porcelain plates, and drank golden wine from crystal goblets. Then they retired to bed.

The next morning, in their bedchamber, Bluebeard said, "Where are my keys, beloved?"

And the Bride answered, "Here, on the ring that you left with me." She took the keyring out of an embroidered casket and handed it to her husband.

"Where," said Bluebeard in a hoarse whisper, "is the smallest silver key?"

"It must have fallen from the ring," said the Bride. "I will look again in the casket."

There was nothing to be done. She handed the key to her husband.

"It is stained with blood," he said, and to his wife it seemed as though the dark waves of his beard were shaking with his rage. "You opened the door of the locked room, and your punishment will be to join those women whom you found there." For a moment, he was silent, then he smiled. "I will kill you with my own sword and place you with the others."

The Bride threw herself before him and pleaded for her life. Her tears and cries would have moved another man to pity, but Bluebeard said only, "You must die and die quickly."

"Only give me leave to pray for a while," said the Bride at last. "Then kill me if it will make you happy."

"I shall give you an hour," said Bluebeard and left the bedchamber. The Bride flew along the corridors to her sister's apartments.

"Sister Anne," she cried. "Our brothers are coming here today. Go to the South Tower and see if you can see them. Signal to them to make haste, I implore you, for I must be killed before the next hour strikes."

Anne climbed to the top of the South Tower and every few moments the poor Bride called to her, "Sister Anne, Sister Anne, what do you see?"

Over and over again, Anne called down, "Only the gardens and the sea beyond," until the Bride was frantic with dread.

At last the clock struck the hour, and Bluebeard came to where his Bride was weeping at the foot of the Tower steps.

"Here is my sword, drawn and ready," he said, and took his Bride by the hair.

"Sister Anne, Sister Anne, what do you see?" she cried, and Anne answered at last, "Two horsemen . . . I see two horsemen."

"Come, Madam," said Bluebeard. "It is time to make our way to the North Corridor. It is time for us to open the black door."

He began to drag his Bride through the palace. Suddenly there came such a banging at the gate, that Bluebeard was surprised and let go of his wife's arm.

The Bride's two brothers, both brave soldiers in the service of the King, raced to Bluebeard's side and killed him with their silver daggers before he had time to say a single word.

Bluebeard had no children, so the Bride inherited his wealth and lands. She arranged a prosperous and happy marriage for her sister, and she gave fine gifts to each of her brothers. She also saw to it that Bluebeard's poor dead wives were decently buried, and she set a cypress tree to grow beside each grave.

THE GIRL WHO STEPPED ON A LOAF

~

When Inga was born, she was a beautiful baby and she grew into a child so lovely that everyone in the village came to look at her and wonder. This beauty, however, did not reach as far as her soul, for Inga was a cruel, vain, selfish creature whose favourite games were pulling wings off flies, and cutting worms into little pieces.

Later, as she grew older, she enjoyed such pastimes as capturing butterflies in the meadows and watching their wings flutter and grow still in tightly-closed glass jars. Then she pinned them to a board with silver pins and said, "You are very splendid, little butterflies, but alas, not nearly as splendid as I am!"

Her mother, who was a poor woman, never dared to cross this wilful daughter. Her father had died even before his child was born, so Inga did exactly as she pleased and no one ever scolded her or told her how wicked she was growing.

On her fourteenth birthday, she was sent to work for a wealthy couple who lived in the town. They cared for her as though she were their own daughter, and gave her clean, pretty clothes to wear, and fine shoes to put on her feet.

After Inga had been working in their house for a year, her mistress said to her, "My dear, do you not think it is time you returned to visit your mother? She must be missing you dreadfully."

Inga sighed and grumbled, but in the end she agreed to go, comforting herself with thoughts of how everyone in the village would exclaim when they saw how grandly she was dressed, and how very pretty she looked in her feathered bonnet.

When she arrived at the village, she spotted her mother sitting on a bench some distance away, laughing and talking with some of her friends. Inga shuddered and turned away and began to walk back towards the town.

"I cannot possibly be seen talking to a ragged, dirty old woman like that!" she said to herself. "Her blackened nails, her holey shoes, her mud-splattered skirts and torn petticoats . . . Ugh! I should die of shame and disgust if I so much as approached her."

Her employers were surprised to see her back so soon and suspected that she had never visited her mother at all, but they said nothing.

Another six months passed and once again her mistress came to Inga and said, "See, Inga, I have baked a special loaf for your mother. It is a very long time since you visited her. Take her this loaf, now that the autumn is here. She will be glad of it in the colder weather."

Inga put on her fur-trimmed cloak, and a brand-new pair of shiny leather shoes, which filled her heart with happiness.

"How small and dainty my feet look in these delightful shoes. How elegantly I walk when I wear them! They are the most perfect shoes in the whole world."

She took the loaf from her mistress and set out. It was a large, golden, heavy loaf and from it rose the wonderful smell of new bread. Inga looked very carefully at the path ahead of her, and trod warily for she wanted to keep her new shoes clean at all costs.

When she came to the marsh, the path across it was muddy and wet, but by taking great care with every footstep, Inga had almost managed to reach the other side when suddenly, an enormous puddle spread out before her, too wide to cross in a single step.

Inga did not hesitate. "I shall use this loaf as a stepping-stone," she thought, and threw it into the puddle. She put one foot on the loaf, and lifted the other ready to jump to dry ground, when the bread beneath her began to sink. Down and down into the marsh it went, and Inga's foot was stuck to it, and she was drawn down with it, through the black marsh water, and right into the Marsh-wife's kitchen.

The water of the puddle closed over Inga's head, and no one saw her feathered bonnet, nor her fur-trimmed cloak nor her fine, new, shiny shoes ever again. An old man, who was passing near the marsh while Inga was crossing it, saw exactly what happened and spread the story through the surrounding countryside.

Meanwhile, the Marsh-wife (who is sister to the Erlking) was delighted to have a visitor. Inga was not so happy, for the Marsh-wife's kitchen is a foul-smelling place, where she brews grey beer in reeking barrels, which stand in

slimy mud. Horrid toads and marsh-serpents slip between the barrels and spit their venom into whatever the Marsh-wife is cooking.

"You have come on visiting-day, to be sure," said the Marsh-wife to Inga, "for the Devil's own grandmother is here. Say how-do-you-do at once, child."

Inga wrinkled her nose and said, "How-do-you-do," with a bad grace. The Devil's grandmother had an enormous handbag beside her chair. "She looks like nothing so much as a bony old skeleton dressed in lace," thought Inga. "How horrible her thin white fingers are, and what can she be making?"

The Devil's grandmother knew what Inga was thinking. Her teeth rattled as she laughed and said, "I am weaving a blanket of lies big enough to cover the whole world. When it is finished, I shall embroider it with the French knots of misery and the cross-stitches of misunderstanding. I will make it in the colours of Death and War. . . Oh, black and red never go out of fashion!"

Inga shivered. But the old lady continued, "You, my dear, are a pretty little thing."

Inga nodded. It seemed that the Devil's grandmother had good taste and could recognize beauty when she saw it.

"I shall take you to my grandson's kingdom, where you will make an impressive statue. I see you standing in the Outer Corridor."

That was how Inga found herself turned as stiff and cold as marble, with the loaf she had trodden on still stuck to the soles of her shoes. She could move her eyes and nothing else at all, but that was enough to show her that her fine cloak was muddy and stained, and that slimy creatures she had no names for were creeping in and out of her skirts. She was standing in Hell's Outer Corridor, which had no end and no beginning, and which was crowded with tormented souls, longing to make their way towards the light, whose feet were bound in cobwebs as strong as iron chains, spun by the Devil's own spiders.

There were flies in plenty in this kingdom, too, but the ones that came to Inga were those whose wings she had pulled off years ago. Now they were crawling over her face and she was powerless to prevent it.

She grew hungrier and hungrier, for she could not bend down and eat the golden loaf at her feet. The worst anguish of all, however, was that she could hear every word that was being spoken about her on earth. She knew that her mother was weeping for her, and every tear her mother shed fell on Inga's brow and scalded her.

"Oh, Inga, your pride and vanity have brought you to this! How badly you have treated your poor mother!"

Her master and mistress in the town were also grieving, for they had loved her, but they, too, said, "Oh, Inga, if only you had not been so selfish and so vain!"

Mothers sang songs to their daughters at bedtime about the silly girl who stepped on a loaf and was punished by being drowned in the marsh.

"I cannot bear to hear these things any more," said Inga to herself. "Is there no one in the world to say a good word for me?"

It seemed that there was not.

Years passed. Inga's mother died and the tears she shed for Inga on her deathbed fell on her daughter's head and scorched her hair, but still Inga remained frozen and hungry; still she stood in the Devil's Outer Corridor with the screams of the damned echoing in her ears.

Then, one day, Inga heard her name spoken on earth again. Someone was telling her story to a little girl. The child listened, and at the end of the tale she said, "Oh, poor, poor Inga! Will she never come back to this world again?"

"Never," said the nurse, and the little girl burst into tears.

"Even if she says she is sorry and will never do such things again? Oh, I

wish she could! If poor Inga would only come back, she could have my very best doll to play with."

"I fear," said the nurse, "that Inga is too wicked ever to be forgiven."

The child wept bitterly, and her tears fell on Inga like a cooling shower of rain and melted her heart a little so that she wished she could cry too.

"But I cannot," she said. "I cannot weep, and that is the worst of all my torments."

After many years, the child who had been the only person in the world ever to call her "poor Inga" and not "wicked Inga" or "selfish Inga" or "vain Inga" grew old and died, and on her deathbed, once again, she wept for the luckless girl who had stepped on a loaf and who had stood for so long just outside the very pit of Hell. These tears fell on Inga's shoulders and warmed her frozen limbs a little.

When the old lady was dead, she became one of God's angels, and when an angel asks forgiveness, that forgiveness is granted. Inga felt light fall on her. She felt her limbs soften and shrink and soon she had become a small, brown bird, and was allowed to fly up and up through all the layers of the Underworld until she reached the green earth she thought she would never see again.

The bird that was once Inga thought, "I am unworthy of such happiness. I am unworthy of these trees and this high, blue sky. I have no voice to sing praises with, so I shall hide in cracks and crevices and seek whatever I can find to eat."

The little bird ate what she could, for she had to feed the hunger of many years. Gradually, her voice returned to her, but it was nothing but a tiny cheep-cheep.

When winter came, every lake and pond was frozen to a solid sheet of ice, and snow covered every leaf and rooftop. The little bird flew from place to place, and wherever she found crumbs, she called with her small voice to all the other birds, and they flocked to her side and ate what they could.

All through the winter, the bird flew about finding food for other creatures, until the time came when she had collected as many crumbs as there had once been in the loaf Inga had stepped on.

On that day, exhausted from her labours, the brown bird settled herself to sleep on a sheltered windowsill, and when she woke and spread her wings, they stretched and spread and grew wide and white as snow. This new and shining bird flew up and up towards the clouds; up and up towards the yellow sun that hung like a golden fruit in the pale, wintry sky.

SOMETHING MORE . . .

One morning at dawn, a poor fisherman dragged his net to the shore and found, tangled up in it, a most beautiful fish.

"Your scales are silver and pearl," said the fisherman. "You are the noblest fish I have ever seen, and I must return you to deep waters."

"I give you thanks," said the fish. "I am no sea creature, but an enchanted prince, and if I am the noblest of my kind, then surely you have more goodness in you than most men."

The fisherman helped the beautiful fish to slip again into the quiet waves, and then he returned to his home.

The fisherman and his wife lived in a hovel. There were holes in the roof, the windows lacked glass, and the walls were black with smoke from the fire.

"There was something wondrous in my catch today," said the fisherman to his wife. "An enchanted prince in the shape of a beautiful fish. I put him back into the water and he was full of gratitude."

"Dolt!" said the fisherman's wife. "You could have asked a favour in return. Perhaps this fish is powerful as well as beautiful. Finish your porridge and get down to the shore and summon him." She sighed. "I was cursed with a fool for a husband, a man who cannot see good fortune when it sits on the end of his nose. Ask the fish for a pleasant cottage."

The fisherman went down to the water's edge. The waves rolled over the sand, and beyond the breakers, the sea moved and murmured quietly. The fisherman said:

> *"Beautiful fish*
> *come to the shore.*
> *My wife has a wish*
> *for something more."*

The fish rose up on the crest of the next wave and landed at the fisherman's feet. The fish said:

> *"Tell me what you heard her say.*
> *I shall listen and obey."*

The fisherman hung his head.
"She would like a cottage in which to live."

The fish plunged back into the waters, and the fisherman made his way home, thinking, "Well, I have asked, and even if the fish cannot work a miracle, I can do no more."

When the fisherman arrived at the place where his hovel used to be, there was the prettiest cottage he had ever seen, with a little kitchen garden at the back of it, and a little flower garden at the front.

"Come and see!" shouted his wife from the door. "It is exactly what I dreamed of! I even have a dresser with four and twenty plates displayed upon it! What a fine time we shall have here, beloved!"

For some days, the fisherman's wife was happy in her new home, but one day she said to her husband, "I should have asked for a palace, while I had the chance. Get down to the sea at once, husband, and summon the beautiful fish. If he can do so much, perhaps he can do more. The grandest of all palaces is what I require."

The fisherman went down to the water's edge. A wind blew off the water, and the clouds were grey and low. He said:

> *"Beautiful fish*
> *come to the shore.*
> *My wife has a wish*
> *for something more."*

The fish was there before him in an instant, saying:

> *"Tell me what you heard her say.*
> *I shall listen and obey."*

The fisherman blushed for shame.

"She would like a palace in which to live."

The fish plunged back into the water and the fisherman made his way home. His cottage had gone when he arrived and in its place was the most magnificent palace imaginable.

"How delightful this is!" cried the fisherman's wife. "I have four and twenty bedrooms, a ballroom, a gallery, a scullery, and a table in the banqueting hall set with gold and silver dishes. What a fine time we shall have here, beloved!"

In a few days, however, the fisherman's wife began to complain again.

"A palace is of no use," she said, "without the power to go with it. Get down to the sea at once, husband, and summon the beautiful fish. I want to be the king."

"Ladies are usually queens," said the fisherman.

"Queens are not as powerful as kings," said his wife. "A king and only a king is what I wish to be."

The fisherman went down to the water's edge. The sea was angry and dark, rolling and heaving from the shore to the horizon under a copper sky. The fisherman said:

> *"Beautiful fish*
> *come to the shore.*
> *My wife has a wish*
> *for something more."*

The waves rose up and up and the fish crashed on to the sand, saying:

"Tell me what you heard her say.
I shall listen and obey."

The fisherman stared down at his feet.

"She wants to be king."

The fish plunged back into the water and the fisherman made his way home. There were four and twenty soldiers standing guard outside the palace, and the rooms were full of courtiers, in rustling robes. His wife was sitting on an enormous golden throne, wearing a crown studded with rubies and emeralds the size of pigeons' eggs.

"Bow down before me," she said to her husband, "and kiss the hem of my gown. From now on, you must call me 'Your Majesty' or I shall fling you into my deepest dungeon."

The fisherman's wife enjoyed being king, but it was not enough for her.

"I should like," she said to her husband, "to be the leader of all the churches in the world, and tell everyone how to organize their prayers and ceremonies."

The fisherman went down to the water's edge. Zigzags of lightning cut across the sky, and thunder sounded in the west. The sea was black and furious, and the waves made such a terrible noise as they broke on the shore that the fisherman's words were almost lost:

"Beautiful fish
come to the shore.
My wife has a wish
for something more."